A Legacy for Lara

By Rachel M. Hay

Edited by Pamela Evans

Dedicated to Daisy W. and all the older godly men and women who influenced me early on in my life

Scripture taken from the NEW AMERICAN STANDARD BIBLE®, Copyright © 1960, 1962, 1963, 1968, 1971, 1972, 1973, 1975, 1977, 1995 by The Lockman Foundation. Used by permission.

Chapter One

As Lara James approached Room 26, a smile spread across her face. Although the rain was drumming loudly on the roof above her, she knew that in this room there would be sunshine. It was always that way when she came to visit Daisy Jenkins.

Lara knocked lightly on the open door of the long room, which was divided by a curtain into two living spaces. The front portion of the room belonged to Daisy; the back had belonged to Madge. The walls were covered with floral wallpaper that had faded over the years. Lara suspected that the flowers portrayed had once been red; now they were pink.

Daisy was waiting for Lara and quickly wheeled over to welcome her. Lara was always made to feel like a special visitor, even though she came to see Daisy every Wednesday.

"Sit yourself down," Daisy said warmly, pointing to the only chair in the front of the room. Lara settled herself comfortably for "a chat" with Daisy. In the midst of their conversations, Lara often forgot about the difference in the years between them. Somehow it just didn't seem to matter.

"How are you doing?" Lara asked the older woman. She noticed that Daisy's gray eyes seemed more cloudy than usual. Lara was pretty sure that Daisy had been crying.

"Oh, I'm pushing along," Daisy said. Lara could tell that her words were forced. "I do miss Madge though."

Lara nodded. She imagined that it must be lonely for Daisy now that her roommate had passed away.

A Legacy for Lara

"I miss the sound of her knitting needles," Daisy admitted. "She was always knitting and it seemed like her needles were clinking around the clock."

"She never seemed to speak much when I visited," Lara said, "but it does feel so quiet without her." Lara had enjoyed getting to know Madge during her visits with Daisy and had been the recipient of more than one knitted item of apparel.

"Well, yes..." Daisy's words trailed off along with her thoughts. For a minute or two, neither woman spoke. Then Daisy turned to Lara again. "How are things going with you?"

"Pretty well," Lara said. "Colin's taking me out tonight for our one year anniversary as a couple." Lara was surprised at how casually she had said the words. The truth was, she had been thinking of nothing else for the last few weeks.

"So it's been a year already, hmm?" Daisy asked. Lara nodded, smiling. Daisy had a way of repeating something when she was thinking. It had taken Lara a little time to get used to, but she appreciated it now as a reminder that Daisy was really listening.

"What are your plans?" Daisy asked with a twinkle in her eye. "Or do you know?"

"Colin is taking me to the restaurant we went to on our first date," Lara answered. She shrugged her shoulders. "We've eaten there a few times since. I guess it's just comfortable to us."

"And how is your relationship? Is that comfortable?" Lara felt Daisy's penetrating gaze on her without looking up. Daisy certainly didn't mind asking the tough questions.

Lara hesitated before responding. This was what she had been considering for some time. Her relationship with Colin was comfortable *now*, but she knew that Colin was anxious for change. He had spoken about it recently, hinting that he was ready and willing to pop the question if only he were sure of the answer he'd receive.

"Colin and I get along really well," Lara began. "I don't think I've ever met a nicer man, but…"

"You aren't sure you trust him enough to marry him?"

Lara had been looking around the room, but now she instinctively looked at Daisy. Lara wasn't sure she liked the way that Daisy had summarized her reservations, but she knew that Daisy only meant to help. Lara could trust her. Over the last several years, Daisy had earned her trust. But it had taken time and Lara wasn't sure everyone could be as patient as Daisy… especially Colin.

"I'm trying to, but it's complicated." Lara answered at length.

"Most things in life are, honey," Daisy said in her gentle way. Lara couldn't help but smile. While Daisy's words weren't exactly encouraging, the very fact that she was sitting here cheerfully after all she had been through gave Lara hope.

Lara looked across from Daisy to her small writing desk. The items on it never moved, and it was a comfort to Lara to see the same antique lamp, open Bible, and family photos. Prominent among the group was a framed black and white picture of Daisy's late husband.

"Can I ask you a question?" Lara asked.

"I'm all ears," Daisy said.

"How did you know that Reg was the right man for you?" Lara often asked Daisy for advice, but she generally shied away from asking personal questions. She hoped Daisy wouldn't mind this once. The serene smile on Daisy's face put Lara's fears at ease.

"Well, we had known each other since we were kids," Daisy began. "I was 'sweet on him', as we used to say, from the time I was eight years old. He never thought of me as anything more than 'Lucy's friend' for a long time."

"Who was Lucy?" Lara asked.

"She was my best friend when I was a girl," Daisy said. "She was also his little sister."

"So when did he first 'notice you'?" Lara asked. She had heard bits and pieces of Daisy's story over the years, but apparently there were details she had never been told.

"I was about sixteen and I was singing with the choir. I had a special piece to sing with the choir supporting me. I was so nervous, but when I saw him watching me, I was resolved to sing my heart out. We were married two years later."

She was eighteen? Lara thought. *It's been almost a decade since I was that age!*

"Thank you for telling me," Lara said. "I've always been afraid to ask you questions that may hurt you, but I really appreciate you sharing this."

"It doesn't hurt to talk about Reg," Daisy said. "Those were happy memories. The pain will always be there, whether I talk about it or not. I think it's better if I do."

Lara nodded in understanding. She was glad that Daisy seemed open to the prospect of sharing more details of her earlier life. There were many questions that Lara had wanted to ask over the years.

"Do you think that you'll get another roommate sometime?" Lara asked, changing the subject.

"I expect I will," Daisy said without much enthusiasm. "No one will replace Madge though."

"No," Lara agreed, "of course not."

Colin Trent walked slowly through the mall, uncertain of whether to head home or spend some more time shopping. He had already accomplished the purpose of his trip, which was to buy an anniversary card and candy for Lara. He wished he could give her more. He wished she were ready. As if on cue, he passed by a jewelry shop. Perhaps he could browse without drawing attention to himself. He knew now wasn't the time to be purchasing a ring, but he felt as if stepping in the store could somehow bring him closer to the future he envisioned with Lara.

He soon saw it was foolish to believe he could look around without being noticed. He looked up to see a young woman smiling at him.

"Can I help you?" she asked him.

"I'm, um, just looking." Colin felt foolish. Why had he made this detour? He was certainly not going to explain to the store employee that he was hoping to propose but that his girlfriend was dragging her feet.

"Well, if you want to look at any of the rings, let me know. All engagement rings are 10% off this weekend."

And likely most other weekends, Colin thought dryly.

"Thank you." Colin tried to remain polite as he said again he had just come to look and quickly made his escape. The last thing he saw was the disappointed look on the face of the saleswoman. He couldn't help but think that her disappointment in not selling a ring couldn't match his own in not feeling confident enough to purchase one.

Later that evening, as Colin walked to Lara's front door, he felt much like he did earlier when looking at rings. While generally frugal in his tastes, he had paid an outrageous price for four, small imported chocolates that were Lara's favorite. He hoped he didn't look too desperate. He knew she had her reasons for being cautious, but he thought the year they had spent together sufficient time to prove himself worthy of her trust. Until just recently he thought their dreams for the future were beginning to align. That was before their last evening out, when he had casually mentioned their future as an almost settled matter. He wasn't even sure why he had said what he did. Perhaps it was just because he had begun to see Lara as a permanent part of his life. Lara had drawn back at the time and changed the subject.

Colin considered how long he had waited for this relationship. Many of his friends were married with young children. Colin had never met anyone he really cared for until Lara. He knew time was precious and he didn't want to spend more of his life waiting, but he couldn't imagine his future without Lara.

Colin's thoughts were cut short as Lara opened the door and smiled at him. She was wearing a knee-length hunter green dress and black high heels. She had curled her brown hair so it framed her face, and had obviously taken more pains with her makeup than she did ordinarily. Colin stood still for a moment, just enjoying the sight of her.

"Ready to go?" he asked at last.

"What do you think?" she asked with a smile.

Although Lara had ordered her favorite pasta dish, she couldn't seem to do more than give the pretence of eating it. She and Colin had talked about various subjects during their drive to the restaurant and their meal thus far, but so cautiously that Lara couldn't remember anything of consequence being said. She debated within herself whether or not to bring up the subject that they were both avoiding. Surely talking about it couldn't be as bad as not talking about it.

"You're awfully quiet this evening," Colin remarked casually. Lowering his voice he said, "I have a feeling it has something to do with what I said last week."

Lara nodded, embarrassed that she was so easy to read.

"Why don't we take a walk and talk about some things after dinner?" Colin asked. His words reminded Lara of one quality she had always admired in him. He was quick to develop a plan when necessary for solving a problem. *Too bad* I'm *the problem,* Lara thought dryly.

"I'd like that," Lara said.

After Colin had left the waiter a generous tip, he led Lara outside. The restaurant was situated in the middle of an outdoor shopping center with broad walks and benches spaced out beneath spreading trees. Colin spied an empty bench a distance away from any other shoppers, and, holding Lara's hand, he led her to it. The night air was cool, but refreshing after the heat of the day. After they had sat down, Lara wrapped her arms around herself, more to calm her nerves than to warm herself.

"Cold?" Colin asked.

"Not exactly," she said.

"So, I've been wondering," Colin said slowly, "have you given any more thought to our last conversation?"

"Yes," Lara answered, "quite a lot."

"I'm not even sure I remember what I said now," Colin said, "but I remember how you reacted. What was it that bothered you?"

Lara looked at Colin's puzzled expression and wished she could instantly resolve this matter between them. She hated to cause pain to anyone, and she cared deeply for Colin. She knew her words would pain him, at least for now, but she didn't know how to avoid it.

"I wasn't ready for you to talk about our future the way you did," Lara said. She avoided meeting Colin's gaze. It was the only way she could finish what she had to say. "I'm so thankful for this past year and all the time we've spent together. It's been the best year of my life. I'm just not ready for anything to change... yet."

Colin listened attentively while Lara spoke. He knew from experience that Lara wasn't a flatterer. He trusted she meant every word she said. For a moment he delighted in her words. Then the same familiar pang returned.

"And when do you think you might be ready?" he asked. He'd tried to mask his impatience, but wasn't sure he'd succeeded.

"I don't know... exactly," Lara said with hesitation. "How long does it take to trust something that's so different from what you knew as a child?"

Colin didn't answer in words, but he put his arm around Lara's shoulder and waited.

"My parents didn't even seem to like each other for most of my childhood," Lara explained. "They argued and wouldn't speak to each other for days on end. The silence was... suffocating."

"I know all that," Colin said. "You've told me many times." Mindful of the look on Lara's face, Colin quickly amended his words. "But I'm not opposed to talking about it again."

"I'm just afraid, I guess," Lara admitted. "I don't want my children to grow up the way I did."

"But your parents weren't Christians then, Lara," Colin gently reminded her. "We're both believers. We'd be starting out on a whole different playing field."

"You always think of sports, don't you?" Lara teased, hoping to soften the mood of their conversation.

"They have a lot to teach us," Colin answered honestly.

"I just need a little more time." Lara hated to even ask it, but she had to. "Can you give me a little more time?"

Lara couldn't help but notice how slowly Colin exhaled before responding.

"I'll try to be patient," he said, "and I'll keep praying for you."

"Thank you," Lara answered. It was all she could say. She just hoped it was enough.

Chapter Two

The next few days were busy ones for Lara. As a photographer, she had learned from experience that certain seasons of the year were more demanding than others. She spent Thursday, Friday, and Saturday, taking more senior pictures than she dared to count. Every evening she came home worn out and wanting nothing more than to eat a quiet dinner and get some extra sleep.

She had a short phone conversation with Colin, but didn't see him again until church on Sunday. He had saved her a seat next to him, which she found a few minutes before their pastor came forward to give the announcements.

"Glad you made it," Colin whispered to Lara.

"Barely," Lara said. "Sorry I'm late."

"I'm just glad that you're here," Colin said, smiling.

Lara smiled back at him, then she turned her attention to the bulletin she was holding. She appeared engrossed in its contents. The next thing Colin knew, Lara had retrieved a pen from her purse and was scribbling something underneath the date at the top of the bulletin. He leaned over her shoulder to read, *Mail Dee's card ASAP!*

Lara noticed Colin reading her reminder to herself. Since the sanctuary was now silent, she scribbled another note underneath the first one. *Belated…again.*

Lara was surprised when Colin took her pen from her hand and wrote his own message. *It's OK.* ☺

13

Lara did smile as directed, but inwardly she knew that it wasn't okay. Dee was her only sister. Despite their differences, Lara wanted Dee to know that she thinking about her on her birthday. *Why do I seem to be running late for so many things these days?* Lara asked herself.

"So how was your date with Colin?" Daisy asked almost immediately when Lara came to visit her the following week. Daisy looked at Lara with such keen interest that Lara felt sorry she hadn't communicated this news earlier. Daisy's generation often missed out on the instant communication the rest of the world seemed to enjoy. Maybe Lara should have called Daisy days ago.

"Oh, it went all right," Lara said vaguely.

"What does that mean exactly?" Daisy asked, obviously not satisfied with Lara's answer.

"Well, we talked about how I need some more time before making a serious commitment." Lara's words sounded lame to her own ears. She wondered what Daisy thought of them. "I feel so selfish asking Colin to give me more time," Lara said, her reserve now slipping away. "But I'm not trying to be selfish; I'm trying to be cautious. Isn't that a good thing?"

Daisy was silent for a time. Lara listened to the seconds tick by on the large grandfather clock that sat just outside Daisy's room.

"Caution is good, yes…" Daisy began. Lara knew that Daisy would understand. She almost said so before she realized that Daisy had not finished what she meant to say. "But there is such a thing as being too cautious."

"What do you mean?" Lara asked.

"Well, I will say that love has its risks," Daisy admitted. "But not loving has its risks too. We are all going to get old." Daisy glanced across at Lara and smiled. She remembered being her age. It didn't seem such a long time ago. "Trust me on this one. Growing old with the one you love is a great blessing." Daisy looked across at the picture of her husband, Reg. Tears began to pool in her eyes. "And when the Lord calls one of you home, the other will still have... the memories."

Lara didn't quite know what to say, so she sat silently for a time. She wasn't exactly sure why Daisy had mentioned growing old. It wasn't something Lara thought about much at her time in life.

It wasn't until Lara got into bed that night that she realized the implication of Daisy's words. When Daisy had spoken about the risks of not loving and growing old, she had meant to subtly warn Lara that if she waited too long she might lose Colin. She might spend her life alone. Lara had been so focused on her fears that she hadn't taken the time to consider this. It was too much to think about just now. Turning off the lamp, Lara pulled her comforter under her chin. Sleep, however, was a long time in coming.

Dee James rarely hesitated. She usually knew what she wanted and, when it was in her power, worked hard to achieve it. But people weren't like exams or exercise goals. They responded to your attempts to conquer them and didn't always give you the chance. All week Dee had wrestled with the idea forming in her mind. Should she or shouldn't she invite herself to visit her sister, Lara, on the other side of the country? She had a convenient excuse. Her good friend, Marcia, had invited her on vacation with her family. They were going to stay in a cabin not thirty miles from where Lara now lived. Marcia was an only child and her parents had generously offered to cover the cost of Dee's plane ticket. They also encouraged Dee in her scheme to spend some time with Lara if possible.

Dee knew part of the reason for her hesitation was pride. After all, Lara had been the one to choose a college and later a home far away from the rest of the family. While this in itself wasn't a crime, Dee knew Lara had done it deliberately to remove herself from the troubles at home. She had left her little sister in the midst of a difficult situation and seemed to largely forget about her.

Lara seemed to think that her family's situation was hopeless, but it wasn't. Not a year after Lara left for college, Dee and both her parents' lives were drastically changed. Lara knew this and yet she still kept them all at arm's length. She visited with her family over the holidays, but was always reserved and obviously uncomfortable around them. Dee remembered asking Lara once herself if she had forgiven her parents. Lara had been quick to claim she had, but Dee was skeptical. Surely forgiveness as God intended it didn't mean keeping someone so far away they could never hurt you again.

Dee knew her dilemma was similar to her sister's. She could pick up the phone and call Lara, only to have her invent some excuse why the timing of their visit wouldn't work. Or maybe Lara would have a legitimate reason. Either way, Dee knew she would be hurt and it would be hard to forget. Still, she picked up the phone...

Lara reached to answer her ringing phone, but paused when she saw the caller ID. It was her sister. Dee hadn't called her in a long time and Lara wondered what had prompted this call. She hoped that nothing was the matter with either of her parents. *Stop being so negative,* Lara reprimanded herself, before running through the list of other possibilities in her mind. It wasn't quite time for her family's reunion yet, but she supposed Dee could be calling about it. Suddenly Lara realized that the call was going to be transferred to voicemail if she didn't pick her phone up quickly.

"Hello?" she answered.

"Hey, Lara! It's Dee!"

Lara was encouraged by the cheery intonation of her sister's voice.

"Dee! How are you?"

"I'm fine. How are you?

"I'm fine." Lara felt like this was some kind of lame script that they rehearsed every time they spoke to each other. She was trying to think of something intelligent to say, when Dee chimed in.

"I have a proposal for you," Dee explained.

Lara waited with interest to hear what Dee would say next. Her little sister was never one for beating around the bush.

"How would you like me to come for a visit?"

Lara was certainly surprised at her sister's question. She wasn't sure what had prompted it and was thankful when Dee continued to tell about Marcia's family vacation and her role in it.

"When would you be coming?"

"On the eighth of next month. We could meet at some place you suggest and then you could drive me back to your apartment. I can stay for three days; then I'll need to get back for school."

"I think..." Lara's words trailed off. What did she think? What would her energetic sister think of her if she saw her in her natural habitat? While Dee was at a distance, Lara could at least keep up an appearance of having an exciting life. There was a certain romance to being a photographer after all. And then there was Colin. What would Dee say about him? Worse yet, what would she say *to* him? She would have to have him over while Dee was staying with her.

"I think that would be fine." Lara hoped it *would* be fine. She felt it would be wrong to close this door that her sister had graciously opened. She knew how Colin and Daisy would both advise her if she had time to ask them. "I'll let you know what restaurants I like in town and you can choose one. I'll meet you there."

"Great!" Dee sounded positively cheerful. "And will I get to see Colin while I'm there?"

Lara let out a little sigh. She was in for it now.

"So your little sister is coming for a visit?" Daisy asked with interest. She knew that Lara and her sister were not what could be called close. Dee had been going to college on the other side of the country. The physical distance accounted for some of the separation between the sisters, but Daisy wondered what other causes might have kept them apart.

"It will be an interesting couple of days," Lara admitted.

"Can I ask why you two haven't been closer?" Daisy asked gently. "I know I'm probably interfering, but things look different from where I'm at in life. Family is so important."

Inwardly Lara cringed. She knew Daisy had a point. She should have kept in better contact with Dee.

"Well," Lara began, "Dee's a lot younger than I am. She was still a girl when I went to college. We're really different. She loves to talk and she's very... perky." Lara had been speaking seriously, so when Daisy began to laugh, Lara felt a trifle annoyed.

"And when has perkiness been a crime?" Daisy asked.

"It's not," Lara said cautiously. "Only, I wish I could bounce back from things the way she does."

"So you envy her perkiness?" Daisy asked.

"In a way, I guess I do." Lara smiled, but it was a dreary sort of smile.

"Why don't you bring her here to visit me?" Daisy asked, changing the subject. "You know how I love to have visitors."

Lara's smile became genuine. If anyone could help her during her visit with Dee, it would be Daisy.

When Lara saw Colin at church on Sunday, she told him about her sister's upcoming visit.

"Do you remember meeting Dee at my mom's surprise birthday party?" Lara asked. Colin smiled as the memory came to him.

Although he and Lara had only been dating for a little over a month, Colin was feeling very optimistic about their relationship and he hadn't wanted to pass up this opportunity of meeting Lara's family. However, surrounded by a sea of relatives and family friends, none of whom he'd ever met before, Colin felt his courage wavering. Lara too seemed shy and ill at ease. She made introductions, but Colin knew it would take weeks for him to learn to match all the names and faces.

Suddenly a young woman came rushing over to Lara and Colin. She was dressed like she was going to a prom and everything she said and did was performed quickly.

After saying something to Lara that Colin failed to overhear, the woman turned to him.

"You must be Colin! It's so good to meet you! I'm so glad you could come! Lara hasn't told us much about you, so you'll have to tell us all yourself. Oh," looking down at her watch, "I have to go speak to someone about the cake. Excuse me. I'll find you later!"

Colin stood speechless for a moment. The woman, whoever she was, knew who he was, but he had failed to learn her identity. Lara helped him out.

"That," Lara said, "was my sister Dee."

"What's so funny?" Lara asked. Colin had failed to answer her question, but instead seemed absorbed in thoughts that he apparently found rather humorous.

"Do you really need to ask if I remember your sister?"

"I guess she is unforgettable," Lara agreed.

As Lara entered the restaurant she had suggested to her sister, she quickly spotted Dee. There were three other people with her that Lara knew must be Marcia and her parents. Lara felt self-conscious about greeting Dee in front of them, but Dee had no such qualms. She pointed Lara out to her friends and left them to greet her sister.

"Lara! It's so good to see you!" Dee said, as she gave her older sister a hug.

"It's good to see you too," Lara answered. "Thanks for making it out to my neck of the woods."

"I'm glad I had such a good excuse," Dee remarked casually. Lara instantly felt a bit of self-reproach. Did Dee feel she had to have a good reason for coming to visit her? She never would have needed to suggest a visit if Lara had been more hospitable.

"Will you introduce me to your friends?" Lara asked, changing the subject.

"Sure thing. We ordered our drinks already and were looking over the menu. What do you suggest?"

The sisters returned to the table and Dee introduced Lara to Marcia and her parents. Lara found it easy to see why Dee and Marcia were friends. Both were eager for conversation and laughed easily. Marcia's parents were more polite in the questions they asked Lara about herself, but Lara still felt ill at ease in their presence.

When the topic of conversation turned to Colin, Lara said as little as possible. She didn't know what Dee had told them about her relationship with him, but she didn't intend to broaden their knowledge if she could help it.

"My sister's a private person," Dee told Marcia, when Lara had failed to answer Marcia's question. "We should probably change the subject."

Lara gave Dee a grateful smile. Clearly her sister knew she had her limits.

After their meal, Dee bade goodbye to Marcia and her parents and followed Lara to her car. Lara was silent for the first several minutes of their drive to her apartment. After spending time in crowded places meeting new people, Lara craved solitude. But happening to glance over at Dee, Lara could tell her sister was anxiously waiting for her to say something.

"Did you have a good time with Marcia and her family?" Lara asked.

"Yes!" Dee answered enthusiastically. "The cabin we stayed in had a hot tub and a great big fireplace. We went hiking several times and then went back to the cabin to relax. It was so nice."

"Where did you meet Marcia?" Lara asked.

"We go to school together. We helped each other survive anatomy last year."

"Is she in the same program you're in?"

"No, Marcia's in the sports medicine program." Lara remembered that Dee was studying to be a personal trainer. Lara could envision her lively sister encouraging and challenging people to work hard to meet their goals.

"So, enough about me," Dee said abruptly. "Let's talk about you!"

Oh no. Here it comes, Lara thought.

"I understand why you didn't want to share details about your personal life with my friend, but *I* am your sister." Dee smiled sweetly at Lara, who was thankful for the excuse of driving to pretend that she didn't see.

"What do you want to know?" Lara asked, trying to assume a calmness she did not feel.

"Do you think you're going to marry him?" Dee asked without blinking.

"You don't waste any time in asking!" Lara was trying to keep her eyes on the road, but it was difficult when she knew she was under the scrutinizing gaze of her sister.

"I don't think we should waste time in life," Dee said simply. "We never know how much we have left."

"It seems strange to hear you talk so serious," Lara answered, avoiding the subject of Colin. "My baby sister has changed quite a bit."

"I'm hardly a baby anymore. In fact, if you don't hurry, I might end up getting married before you do."

Lara was at a loss for words. How many more of these conversations would she have with her sister over the next few days? Thankfully, Lara was just turning into the parking lot of her apartment complex. Ignoring her sister's comment, she helped Dee unload her things and step inside. She knew Dee would be asking more questions soon, but if she could catch her breath before they came, perhaps she would handle them better.

"Welcome to my home," Lara said to Dee as they entered the apartment. "I'll take you on the grand tour. It shouldn't take very long." Lara was finding it easy to talk now that she was back in her familiar environment.

"It looks nice," Dee was quick to comment.

"As you saw on the left as we entered, we have my little office space," Lara said. Lara's computer was surrounded by shelves that held various pictures and keepsakes. Dee seemed to be studying these, apparently looking for things she recognized.

"This picture looks familiar," Dee commented, pointing to a framed photograph of leafy trees with the sunshine breaking through behind them.

"That's because it's from the infamous canoe trip," Lara said. It was nice to know that by just a few words she could communicate a depth of meaning that wouldn't be possible with most people.

"Ah, yes," Dee said, understanding what Lara meant at once. "The trip where I was sure either Mom or Dad was going to swim to shore and leave the rest of us to fend for ourselves."

"That's the one. I remember leaning over the canoe as far as I could to get this picture. I think I would have toppled over the edge if Dad hadn't caught hold of my life vest." Lara smiled. She realized now that she must have been a bit of a trial to her parents at times. She could be so absorbed in preserving reality through pictures that she sometimes failed to be aware of her surroundings.

"I like this picture of the four of us," Dee said, turning Lara's attention to another picture and another memory. Lara remembered being ten on this occasion, which meant that Dee would have only been about three.

"Yeah, that's one of my favorites," Lara said. "Now, shall we continue our tour?" she asked. Dee nodded, wondering when she had last seen Lara looking so relaxed and cheerful.

"Over here is my little living area, where I'll be sleeping while you're here," Lara said. Dee would have liked to have asked questions about Lara's furnishings and tastes in decorating, but she managed to save her questions for later. Lara talked while she walked and Dee followed her around obediently. "Back here we have my kitchen and dining table. Around the corner is the bathroom. And this is my bedroom, where you are going to sleep while you're here. That's about it."

"It's cozy," Dee said. "I've never lived on my own before. I wonder how much I would like it. Do you ever get lonely?"

"Well," Lara said, hesitating, "Sometimes, I guess. I work around people all day long so I'm usually glad to come home where it's quiet. Colin and I get together or call each other most days of the week. But…"

Lara stopped herself. She had been talking without taking much time to consider what she was saying. She knew Dee would be expecting her to finish her sentence.

"But?" Dee was clearly intrigued.

"But, I wouldn't want to live alone forever," Lara admitted.

"Did you get the card I sent you for your birthday?" Lara asked. "I'm sorry it was late."

"Yeah, I got it," Dee said. "But you didn't have to send me a card. You could have just called."

Lara felt awkward. "I don't talk on the phone much," she admitted. "There are always silences when I don't know what to say."

"You don't have to worry about that with me," Dee answered easily. "I can always find something to say to break the silence.

Lara laughed. "I'll remember that for next time."

After helping Dee unpack her things, Lara poured two tall glasses of lemonade. She knew the beverage was her sister's favorite. For a few moments, the sisters were quiet and Lara was lost in thoughts of how much Dee had changed over the last few years. Dee's hair used to hang down her back, but now it brushed her chin. Her clothing was trendy and Dee seemed to exude confidence in the way she carried herself. All in all, Dee was far from the ten-year-old child Lara remembered clinging to her when she left for college. Lara remembered that day vividly; she wondered if the memory was still as fresh in her sister's mind.

Lara had been stacking her last few boxes in the trunk of the family minivan. She had never been more excited. She was finally going to be able to get away from home, from her parents' frequent quarrels. With her leaving, it seemed they argued more than ever. Perhaps they were both on edge because they were going to miss her, but if so, they surely chose strange ways to express their sadness.

Dee, too, had been acting peculiar. She had been quiet much of the last few days. Usually she could be counted on to fill the heavy silences. Lara chose not to think too much about it. If she did, she would only end up feeling sorry for her little sister. She knew she would not want to be in Dee's shoes. But then, she had been in them before. Now it was time for her to move on, to begin a life quite different from the one she had known.

While she was lost in her own thoughts, she barely noticed Dee sneak up behind her at the back of the van.

"Lara?"

Lara turned to see Dee, eyes red and puffy, hair a mess, shoul-

ders sagging. It was enough to make Lara feel guilty and wish she had chosen to go to college locally.

"Yes?" she answered, trying to harden her heart a little. But instead of responding, Dee just threw her arms around her older sister. Lara only hoped Dee couldn't see the tears that were forming in her eyes.

"I'm going to miss you so much," Dee sobbed. "It's going to be so different without you."

"I know," Lara admitted, trying to smooth Dee's disheveled blond locks. She tried to comfort her sister, but avoided empty words that would only hurt worse in the long run.

Soon after, Lara's father told her it was time to leave. She said a quick good-bye to her mother and Dee, before getting into the van for the eight hour journey. She almost didn't look back one last time, but the pull was too strong to ignore. Her last memory was of Dee with tear-stained cheeks, waving at her bravely.

Dee thanked Lara for the lemonade, bringing her moment of reminiscing to a standstill. Lara almost felt that Dee could read her thoughts as she had apparently noticed her mind was elsewhere.

"I'm really glad you came," Lara told her sister. She was surprised at how much she meant it. She admired Dee's courage in suggesting the visit. It was humbling. After all, Dee had come all this way to see *her*. It should have been the other way around. Lara determined, more resolutely than ever, to make Dee feel at home.

"I think I told you about my friend, Daisy," Lara said.

"She's the elderly woman that you visit in the nursing home, right?" Dee responded quickly.

Inwardly Lara winced. Yes, every part of Dee's description of Daisy was true. But this wasn't how Lara thought of Daisy, not in the least. Daisy might be old physically, although Lara hated to admit that much to herself because of the implication that went with it. But her spirit was still young. Lara often didn't even think of Daisy in terms of age at all. She mostly saw her as a good friend whose sound advice had guided her on many occasions. Lara wondered if Dee would be able to see these things in the short time she was here. She hoped she would.

"Yes, I visit her every Wednesday afternoon. When I saw her last week, I told her how you would be coming and she told me she'd like to meet you. Would you mind coming with me to see her while you're here?"

"I'd love to!" Dee answered enthusiastically. She was beginning to feel better about this trip. To Dee, with her easy and open temperament, Lara was still reserved. However, Lara's willingness to introduce Dee to a good friend showed that she was trying to make her feel at home. It was a gentle welcome into her sister's life; and for this, she was grateful.

Chapter Three

As Lara pulled into the parking lot of Daisy's nursing home, her eyes scanned the sweeping front porch carefully. Sure enough, there was Daisy, wheeling herself around the raised flower garden she helped to tend from time to time. She seemed to be lost in thought as Lara and Dee approached her a minute later.

"Daisy, I'd like you to meet my sister, Dee."

"I wouldn't have needed you to tell me she was your sister," Daisy answered with a wide smile. "I can tell by the resemblance. How are you, dear?"

"I'm very well, thank you," Dee answered while reaching out to take Daisy's offered hand.

Lara wondered at Daisy's comment about the similarity between Dee and herself. Daisy knew how Lara compared herself to her sister. Did she really think them alike? Lara knew Daisy would never lie, even to gratify her vanity. The realization was a pleasant one. She liked to think she looked something like her sister.

"Daisy, you appeared to be far away when we arrived. Can I ask what you were thinking of?" Lara hoped her question didn't make Daisy uncomfortable in any way. Daisy's laugh set her mind at ease.

"Well, if you must know, I was thinking about how desperately this flower bed needs to be weeded and how, if I weren't in my Sunday best and waiting for you two dears, I'd be doing just that right now."

Dee smiled broadly at her sister. She could see the attraction in visiting this lady every week. She welcomed the hour ahead with open arms.

"Oh, but I did have another purpose in coming out to meet you," Daisy said suddenly, as if she had just remembered something. "I have a new roommate. And she's..." Daisy hesitated as she searched for the appropriate words, "a little unusual. She's none too happy about being here and she likes to keep to herself. I don't think I've heard her speak more than one word at a time since she came a few days ago."

"Well, I guess you don't have to worry about your room being too noisy," Dee ventured to say. Lara smiled inwardly. Dee always seemed to have a reply to everything.

"That's the thing of it though," Daisy answered. "Before Flo came, the silence was comforting. Now I know someone else is around even if she doesn't say much. It's... strange."

"So her name is Flo?" Lara asked.

"Yes. A name as short as the answers she gives to anything you ask her. Even rhymes with her favorite word: no." Daisy chuckled briefly, then her smile turned sad. "Poor soul. I shouldn't laugh. I just wish she would see that she does herself no favors by cutting everyone else off."

"I'm sure she can't help but be cheered up by being around you," Dee remarked, as confidently as if she had known Daisy for some time. "Even if she doesn't show it."

"Well, that *is* a pleasant thought. Why don't we head inside and then you can meet Flo for yourself?"

Dee looked to be having the time of her life, or so it appeared to Lara.

Inside Room 26, Daisy introduced the two sisters to her new roommate. Flo had been apparently nodding off in her wheelchair when they arrived. She tried to save face by grasping the piece of literature closest at hand. Never mind it was a complimentary magazine apparently placed on her table when she was dozing. She held it upside down in her hands, the back cover showing a young woman with a bright smile which sharply contrasted with the dour expression of the older woman.

"Hello," Dee began at once. "It's good to meet you. I'm Dee James and my sister, Lara, comes to visit Mrs. Jenkins every week, so I expect you'll be getting used to seeing her."

Flo looked Dee and Lara up and down and then made a sort of grunt in reply.

"This appears to be a nice place. How long have you been here?" Dee asked with her friendliest smile.

"Friday."

"What do you think of it?"

Flo shrugged her shoulders. Daisy gave Dee a look of encouragement. She was really glad that Dee was trying to make conversation, despite the meager results.

Lara looked at her sister in wonder. What possessed Dee to try to draw this woman out was beyond her. Then Lara saw the little gleam in Dee's eyes. Flo was a challenge to her. Lara knew it without asking. Dee was trying to see if she could get her to answer her in something resembling a complete sentence. Lara admired her sister's bravery, and wished she had a little more backbone herself.

"I'm sure you enjoy having Daisy as a roommate." Dee paused as she realized that she had failed to ask a question. This really was more difficult than it seemed. "We were looking at the flowers out front. Don't you think they're beautiful?"

"Okay."

"Which flowers are your favorites?"

"Spring."

"Daffodils, crocuses, tulips?"

"All."

Dee sighed. She was through with this game. If Flo couldn't have the decency to answer her civilly, she wouldn't give her the satisfaction of continuing. Daisy suggested they head back outside and the three women made their retreat. None of them stopped long enough to look back at Flo, whose head hung so low she looked like she didn't have a friend in the world.

That evening as Daisy prepared to turn in, she asked Flo what she thought of her young visitors. She only received something like a grunt in response. Daisy's heart went out to her new roommate, who seemed determined to box herself off from the rest of the world.

Feeling a sudden inspiration, Daisy decided to say her evening prayers aloud. After all, since Flo hardly said a word, she wouldn't be likely to protest. Or would she?

"Heavenly Father, Thank you for this day and for the friends with which you have surrounded us." As Daisy paused for breath, she heard Flo cough purposely. She decided to ignore it and keep speaking what was on her heart.

"I thank you for my new friend, Flo. Please help her to settle in well here. Help her to know that she is welcomed and valued. Remind her of Your great love for her, a love so great that it sent Jesus to the cross to pay the penalty for our sins. In His Name, I pray. Amen."

As Daisy laid her head on her pillow, she prayed silently that the words she had said would help Flo. Daisy determined that no matter how much Flo protested, she would have at least one friend in her new home.

Chapter Four

"I really enjoyed our visit with Daisy, even if Flo's company left something to be desired," Dee told her sister that evening. "Now, what do you have planned for tomorrow?"

"I thought I could show you around town, maybe do some shopping." Lara wasn't sure what would interest Dee so she'd only come up with a short mental list of things to do. "There's an outlet mall just out of town that you might like."

"I have a better idea," Dee said enthusiastically, "let's go running!"

"Running?" Lara asked, bewildered. "I haven't gone running in years!" How long had it been? She remembered participating in high school track and field. Had she done nothing since then?

"Well," Dee said, "if you go running with me tomorrow, you'll no longer have that as an excuse the next day. You have to start sometime."

"I guess you're paying attention in class," Lara said teasingly. "I suppose they're teaching you how to persuade people to exercise."

"I prefer to think of it as helping people to feel their best." Dee was now speaking in her professional voice. Obviously this subject was a passion for her and Lara was surprised to see the change in her sister's demeanor. "I think if people knew how good they'd feel if they took better care of themselves, they wouldn't need much encouragement from me."

33

"Okay, you've convinced me," Lara said. "I'll go running with you, but my pace will be slow."

"That's all right," Dee said, happy to have gained her point. "I can jog slowly so you can keep up with me."

Lara smiled. *I'm not sure I'll ever be able to keep up with you*, she thought to herself.

At the end of their run, Lara threw herself down on the grass, utterly worn out.

"Do you have any idea how far we ran?" she asked, in-between breaths. "It felt like a few miles at least."

Dee retrieved her phone from her pocket and checked the distance.

"Actually, it was just over a mile."

"Ugh!" Lara said, clearly disgusted. She could never understand how some people went running for fun. She looked across at Dee, who was breathing heavier than usual, but otherwise appeared no worse for the wear.

"You've been a good sport about running, Lara," Dee said encouragingly. "Why don't we go back and get cleaned up and then have a movie night after dinner? I brought some of my favorites DVDs."

"Well," Lara said, "as much as I would like that, I'm having another dinner guest tonight."

"Who?" Dee asked.

"Colin, of course." Lara enjoyed watching the expression on Dee's face change. Clearly her sister had been waiting for this.

"I can't wait! I only met Colin briefly that one time and he seemed so uncomfortable, he hardly said a word. Of course, you hadn't been dating for long and I guess he was nervous."

A Legacy for Lara

Lara narrowly succeeded in stifling a laugh. Dee sometimes made *her* nervous, and she was her sister.

When Colin arrived at Lara's apartment, he was greeted by both sisters. Dee seemed to be brimming with excitement. Lara was smiling, but Colin thought she appeared a little uneasy.

"Colin, you remember Dee from my mom's surprise birthday party," Lara said by way of introduction.

"Yes," Colin said, reaching his hand out to shake Dee's. "You're hard to forget."

"Should I take that as a compliment?" Dee asked.

Lara was relieved that Colin and Dee were relaxed enough to tease one another. Now if *she* could just take a deep breath, maybe the evening would go better than she'd expected.

Colin and Dee found plenty of things to talk about while Lara put the finishing touches on the dinner she had made. As she was serving, Lara told Colin about the day she and Dee had spent together.

"If I'm moving a little slower this evening, it's because Dee convinced me to go running this morning," Lara told Colin.

Colin looked at Dee with newfound regard.

"Are you a miracle worker?" he asked. Lara gave Colin a scornful glance.

"I used to go running when I was younger," she said in self-defense. "But yes, Dee can be very persuasive."

Dee smiled.

"So tell me a little about your family," Dee said to Colin.

"Well, I'm the youngest. I have an older sister who's married and has a son named Connor. I like to take him on outings with me. My sister's expecting her second child so she's happy to have some time to herself these days."

"How old is he?" Dee asked.

"He's four, going on twelve," Colin answered. "He's full of big ideas and a lot of fun to talk to."

"Yes, he is," Lara agreed. She looked at Colin and smiled. It always warmed her heart to hear Colin talking about his nephew.

Dee was taking in every detail and inwardly asking herself how Lara could be so calm about her relationship with Colin. From all she had seen and heard, Colin was just the man for her sister. She wondered what she could do to help their relationship along and then she remembered a bit of news that her parents had asked her to convey.

"Lara," Dee said, "Mom and Dad wanted me to tell you there's going to be a family reunion in July at the lake house."

"Why didn't they tell me themselves?" Lara took her hand from Colin's and rubbed it on her skirt. She felt suddenly warm.

"Well, you said earlier that I'm very persuasive," Dee remarked. "Apparently I also make a good messenger." Dee then nodded to Colin. "They've invited you too."

"That's kind of them," Colin said, a little unsure what his response should be. "But I'm not family."

Dee watched Colin's face closely. She thought his look clearly said, *Although I wish I were*. She felt it couldn't hurt to give him a little encouragement.

"Well, maybe *not yet*, but they've been hoping to see you again. I think you made a good impression on them the first time you met."

Dee's words caused Colin to wonder and hope. *Had Lara*

confided in her sister? Was she really beginning to think seriously about marriage?

Colin smiled at Lara without saying a word. Lara tried to smile back at him, but Colin could tell she was uneasy.

"Well, I think I've talked enough for one night," Dee said suddenly, noticing the change in the atmosphere. "Colin, it's so good to see you again. I've got a little reading I planned to do. Good night." And then she disappeared around the corner and shut the door.

Lara was at a loss for words. Sometimes her sister was like a whirlwind that you never knew how to be prepared for, coming or going.

"Do you want to sit on the porch before you go?" Lara asked, trying to think of a way for them to have a little privacy. She hoped that Dee would not be listening at the window.

Almost before they had sat down outside, Lara began talking.

"I must apologize for my sister," she blurted out.

"Oh?" Colin tried to appear surprised, but he felt he knew what was coming.

"She can be very... outspoken with her opinions." Lara paused to collect herself and found she couldn't say what she wanted to say.

"You mean what she said about me not being family... *yet*," Colin spoke for her.

"Yes," Lara said, obviously uncomfortable.

"It's okay," Colin said, more because it was expected than because he really meant it. "I figured as much."

"I'm glad my parents invited you to the family reunion,"

Lara said. She was glad to have something to say to change the subject. "You don't have to come though, unless you want to."

"Is there a reason I wouldn't want to come?" Colin asked.

"Oh, I don't know. You know how family reunions are," Lara responded vaguely.

"No, not yours anyway," Colin said honestly.

"Well, we rent a lake house…" Lara began.

"That sounds promising."

"… and have twelve people fighting over two bathrooms."

"That's better than one." Apparently Colin could find a positive side to everything.

"We go rowing until our arms give out…" Lara continued.

"Exercise is good."

"… then we walk by the beach and read and play card games, and eat lots of seafood."

"What's so bad about that?" Colin asked, seeing that Lara had completed her description.

"Nothing," Lara answered. "It's not so much what we do, I guess." She paused as she considered how to explain. "It's just that we're all so different and we don't get along all that well."

"Wouldn't spending time together help you get along better?" Colin wondered.

"That's just the thing. We spend time together *per se*, but we're all doing our different things. And when we're together for meals or on the lake, we don't talk about anything that really matters."

"Do you want that to change?" Colin reached over to take Lara's hand in his. He knew he was entering dangerous territory with his question, but he didn't want to see the woman he loved spend her life wishing her relationship with family was different, but doing nothing to make it happen.

Lara was quiet for a few moments. An exuberant cicada filled the silence.

"I guess I do, although I don't want to have to become someone I'm not."

"I doubt your family wants you to be anyone else." When Lara looked at Colin skeptically, he continued. "Is there any way you can share with them more of what you do? You mentioned that everyone does their own thing on vacation. What do you do?"

"I take lots of pictures when I'm on vacation," Lara said. "I love to capture images of sunsets and sunrises over the lake. No two pictures ever seem exactly alike and I've taken a lot of them. Then I crop them and touch them up in different ways."

"Do you show them to your family while you're working on them?" Colin asked.

"Well, I don't like to show anyone a picture until it's finished. Otherwise, I might get too many suggestions on editing."

"What do you do with past pictures?" Colin asked.

"I make them backgrounds on my computer mostly."

"Well, maybe you can consider making them into gifts or something," Colin suggested. "Isn't that what hobbies are good for?"

"It's not just a hobby, it's my job." Lara knew she was becoming irritable. She just wished that Colin wasn't always the fount of wisdom when it came to dealing with her family. Things weren't as simple as he made them appear. Maybe he would see for himself if he came. Lara did appreciate her parents inviting

Colin. She hoped they would make him feel at home.

"I'm taking Dee to the airport tomorrow," Lara said later as Colin rose to leave. "Do you have plans for Saturday evening?"

"Well…" Colin said, hesitating, "I'm taking Connor to the aquarium Saturday afternoon and my sister invited me to stay for dinner afterward."

"Oh," Lara said. She was a little disappointed, but she hoped Colin didn't notice. She was really glad to see him spending time with his nephew. It struck her afresh that if she married Colin, Connor would become her nephew too. It was a sweet thought.

"I hope you have a good time," Lara said cheerfully. "I'll see you on Sunday, then?"

"Of course," Colin said. "Good night, Lara."

Lara stared into the darkness for some time after watching Colin's car out of sight. She wondered if Dee had really planned on doing some reading or if that had been just an excuse. If the latter were true, she wondered if Dee would have a lot more to talk about now that Colin had gone home.

Chapter Five

"What are you smiling at?" Aaron James had looked up from his magazine to see his wife, Joanne, gazing at the screen of her cell phone. He was pleased to see her looking so happy, but was naturally curious to know what brought her joy.

Seeming to slowly come out of her reflections, Joanne turned her phone around so her husband could see the picture on the screen. Aaron was not surprised to see that she had already made it her background picture. He smiled in affirmation, then turned his attention back to the article he was reading.

"Isn't it wonderful?" Joanne asked a few moments later.

"What?" Aaron asked.

"How our daughters are spending time together," Joanne answered, a little annoyed that her husband wasn't catching on to her train of thought.

"Well, we knew that Dee was headed out to visit Lara. We encouraged her to do it."

"Yes, but they really seem to be enjoying their time together!"

"How can you tell?" Aaron asked. "Have they talked to you much?"

"Dee has texted me some, but just look at their faces in this picture." Joanne studied it again. "It gives me hope."

"Hope of what?" Aaron asked, taking hold of his wife's hand.

"That someday there will be a picture of all four of us like this." Joanne's face clouded with her words.

At this, Aaron laid his magazine down and reached his arm around his wife.

"With God all things are possible," he whispered into her ear.

When Colin returned from his outing with Connor Saturday afternoon, he found his sister, Sarah, looking more rested than when he'd arrived earlier.

"Did you take my advice and get a nap while you could?" Colin asked teasingly.

"Yes," Sarah said. "It helped that Matt said the same thing. I had plenty of things that I wanted to do, but I guess a nap was what I needed most after all. Did you two have a good time?" Sarah looked down at her son as she asked this question.

"Yeah! We saw lots of fish and sharks!" Connor said with enthusiasm.

"Were you scared?" Sarah asked.

"No," Connor answered without hesitation. "Was I supposed to be?"

Sarah laughed and urged Connor to run inside.

"I want to talk to Uncle Colin for a minute alone," she explained.

"Uh oh! Am I in trouble?" Colin asked, looking over at Connor, who looked a little concerned.

"Of course not," Sarah said, smiling. "Connor, run inside please."

Once the door had shut behind the boy, Sarah turned her full attention to Colin.

"I wondered how things are going with you and Lara," Sarah said.

"Is that all?" Colin said, changing the subject. "I thought you were going to tell me you're expecting twins or something."

"*Colin,*" Sarah said with meaning. "I'm your sister and I want to know how things are going in your life... *really.*"

"Things are fine," Colin said vaguely. When he saw that his answer was not going to satisfy his sister, he considered how much he could get by with sharing. "Lara's sister, Dee, was in town earlier this week and I had dinner with her and Lara."

"What's she like?" Sarah asked.

"Very talkative... like someone else I know." Here Colin paused to glance knowingly at Sarah. "She invited me to Lara's family reunion in July."

"Ooh! That sounds interesting," Sarah said. She appeared so energetic now that Colin almost wished he hadn't suggested that she take a nap. "Are you going to go?"

"I think so. I want to spend more time with Lara's family. Lara seems to struggle with relating to her parents and I want to help her if I can."

"Lara should be so grateful for you," Sarah said with obvious pride in her brother's motives. "Do you think she is?" Colin recognized this as Sarah's sly way of asking if he and Lara were getting any closer to getting engaged.

"Why don't you ask her?" Colin replied. He was obviously a little annoyed.

"Colin," Sarah said, her voice suddenly serious, "I really like Lara. But I worry that she's stringing you along. I want you to be happy."

"Have you been talking to Mom?" Colin asked.

"No," Sarah said. "But if I were Mom, I would suggest that you consider being a little distant from Lara for a time. It might help her see how much she cares for you."

"So," Colin said, considering her words, "you think I shouldn't go to the family reunion?"

"I didn't say that," Sarah replied quickly.

"Okay..." Colin was so ready to be finished with this conversation.

"Just think about what I said?" Sarah asked. "I promise not to mention it once we're inside."

For a moment Colin stood speechless. Then, he swiftly opened the front door and led his sister into the house. Sarah was so stunned that she followed him without any show of resistance.

"We're inside," Colin said, smiling.

Dee's scheduled visit went by quicker than Lara had anticipated. Before she realized it, she was driving Dee to the airport to catch her flight back to school. Lara had never handled goodbyes well. She was either afraid of breaking into tears or embarrassed when someone else did. But Dee's departure affected her so much that she found herself dabbing her eyes despite her best efforts. She was really thankful for the coming family reunion at that moment. It was a token of consolation.

"Colin and I will see you in July at the lake," Lara promised as cheerfully as she could.

"I'll be looking forward to it!" Tears were unashamedly coursing down Dee's cheeks. As she turned to go, she was surprised when Lara gave her one last hug goodbye.

Later, as Lara sat in her now silent apartment she wondered how Dee's last memory of her compared to the one she had of leaving for college. Maybe they weren't as different as she had thought.

When Colin was at home that evening, he pondered his sister's words, but he was unable to come to any satisfactory conclusion. How could he establish distance from Lara when he saw her at church every Sunday? Even if he kept away from her at other times, they would be sure to see each other at least once a week. They lived in the same town and frequented the same stores, often unintentionally running into each other. It didn't seem feasible.

He acknowledged that he did want to get Lara's attention, to help her see that he couldn't always be waiting for her. Maybe it would be better to give her some sort of time constraint. But what would he choose? And wouldn't it just seem like he was being impatient and insensitive? Besides, would he really be happy if he broke off his relationship with Lara because she was taking too long in making up her mind about him?

Colin sighed. He wouldn't do anything different. Not yet, anyway.

Lara looked forward to her visit with Daisy more than usual after Dee's departure. She felt a lack that she had not felt before. She hoped that getting back to her normal routine would help.

She stopped outside Daisy's open door and knocked. Daisy's face was turned away from her, but Lara thought she could tell from Daisy's posture that something was amiss. If so, she just hoped she could be a help and not a hindrance.

"Knock, knock." Lara's words and action seem to startle Daisy out of a daydream. After taking a moment to collect her thoughts, Daisy turned to see Lara standing in her doorway. She had forgotten the tears that had pooled in her eyes, but now thought to check them.

"Daisy?" Lara's voice and look were full of concern. Daisy was grateful for her presence, especially today. She turned toward the picture on the table beside her at which she had been looking when Lara walked in. Although she imagined Lara would understand without words, she felt a little explanation would be helpful.

"We would have been married 55 years today." Daisy tried to manage a smile, but it took effort. "Some days are easier than others. I'm afraid today isn't one of them." Daisy paused for a moment, unsure of what to say next. She was thankful for Lara's gifted way of allowing her to speak before jumping in with her own thoughts.

"Maybe you should do something else this afternoon," Daisy said at length. "I'm not sure I'll be the best company."

Instead of responding, Lara came closer and pulled a small wrapped package from her ample sized purse.

"What's this?" Daisy asked puzzled.

"Open it," Lara encouraged, a twinkle in her eye.

Daisy began to tear back the pink and red flowered wrapping paper. When she saw the contents inside the package she didn't know whether to laugh or cry. She did a little of both.

"Chocolate covered cherries!"

"I remembered today was your anniversary," Lara explained. "I know your Reg would have bought them for you if he was still here. I thought I'd buy them… in his place."

A Legacy for Lara

Lara looked carefully at Daisy. She hoped she hadn't presumed too much. She just wanted Daisy to realize how much she cared for her.

"That was very sweet of you," Daisy said at last. Lara could tell that her friend was truly touched and she was pleased. "Of course, you know I can't have any... doctor's orders." Daisy smiled as she said this. Her smile had a remnant of that mischievous look a child uses when trying to snatch a cookie from the cookie jar when no one is watching. Lara sometimes thought she saw a much younger Daisy in those smiles of hers.

"Didn't you see the label on top? They're sugar-free." Now Lara was smiling as she waited for Daisy's reaction. The older woman grinned from ear to ear.

"How do you open this, honey? There's no time like the present!"

Lara and Daisy enjoyed some moments of relative quiet as Daisy enjoyed her candies and Lara looked around in silent reverie. Then Daisy spoke up.

"I had a letter from a friend yesterday. Can you guess who it is?" she asked.

Lara was puzzled. She didn't feel she knew many of Daisy's friends, or at least anyone who would mail her a letter, and she told Daisy so.

"Well, it just happens you do know this person. It's your sister."

"Dee?" Lara asked, surprised.

"Yes. I thought you might like to read it."

Lara accepted the letter Daisy handed her and read it slowly.

Dear Mrs. Jenkins,

I am so glad I was able to meet you during my stay with my sister. You are a charming woman and I can see why Lara comes to visit you every week. I'm almost jealous.

I hope you are doing well. I am cramming every last bit of information into this little head of mine that will fit. Finals are in two days. Pray for me! You are in my prayers.

Your Friend,

Dee James

Lara handed the letter back to Daisy, carefully avoiding eye contact. Her sister was far more thoughtful than she had realized.

"Your sister calls me a 'charming woman'. I have to say, that made my day. I think the same may be said for her, don't you?"

Lara nodded as a smile spread across her face.

"How are things going with Flo?" Lara asked.

"Well, my room is quiet most of the time," Daisy said. "That's not exactly a new thing. Madge was a quiet person, but the silence was peaceful when she was here. Then, after she was gone, there was an empty kind of silence. Now there's an... uncomfortable silence, if you know what I mean."

Lara nodded understandingly, then changed the subject.

"Daisy, why are you so confident?" she asked honestly. "I wish I could be more like you." Daisy pondered the question a moment before responding.

"Well, I guess I've learned to accept how God made me, with all my weaknesses and limitations. It's taken some time. And now..." Daisy smiled as she spoke, "now I'm too old to learn how to be anyone else."

Joanne was busy searching the grocery store aisle, trying

to figure out where the employees had moved the pasta sauce this time. Why couldn't stores just keep their items where you knew to look for them? Probably because they wanted you to buy more things as you looked for the one item you had yet to check off your list.

"Joanne!" A young woman with a toddler in the basket of her shopping cart pulled up alongside Joanne. "I thought it was you. How are you?"

It took Joanne a moment to remember the woman's name. *Shelly? Suzie? Sherry!*

"I'm fine. How are you?" she asked.

"Tired," Sherry replied honestly. "It's been a long day."

Joanne nodded, not quite sure what to say. She hadn't spoken to Sherry much at church, but she knew that she and her husband often attended their Sunday school class.

"I wanted to tell you I enjoy listening to the things you have to say in our class. Your husband seems to listen to you so intently too. It's sweet to watch you together."

Joanne watched as a sort of haze came over Sherry's eyes. Her daughter dropped a toy she had been playing with and Sherry quickly bent over to pick it up for her. When Sherry stood up, Joanne noticed the tears that had begun to pool in her eyes.

"Is something wrong?" she asked with concern. Sherry shook her head.

"No... and yes," she answered ambiguously. "It's just... I see these other couples and how well they relate to each other. I don't know. Somehow my husband and I... we just seem to struggle a lot. You and your husband... you look so happy."

It took a moment for Joanne to understand what Sherry meant. *If you only knew,* Joanne thought to herself. Of course,

Sherry wouldn't know about the struggles she and Aaron had experienced for years before they came to know the Lord. Joanne remembered them all too keenly. She still struggled to forgive herself for the role she played in Lara's decision to distance herself from her family. It had never occurred to her that anyone would look to her as some sort of role model. She was far too inadequate for that.

But you can share what you have learned. Joanne felt the pull, but she tried to ignore it. She wasn't prepared to share so much of her personal history with someone she barely knew. *Don't you wish someone had helped you?*

"I was wondering," Joanne heard herself saying, "if you might be interested in coming over some night. We could have tea, coffee, hot cocoa, whatever you like."

Sherry smiled. "I would like that."

Chapter Six

Lara was surprised when her friend, Tiffany, rushed to see her after church one Sunday. Tiffany was wreathed in smiles and didn't wait long to tell Lara her good news.

"Michael and I got engaged last night!"

Lara was really at a loss for words. Tiffany and Michael were both several years younger than her and had been dating for barely four months.

"That's wonderful… and quick!" Lara responded, before biting her tongue.

"Not everyone needs a long time to know their own mind!" Tiffany was obviously annoyed. She had hoped that Lara would wish her joy instead of criticize her timing. She turned to go, but Lara called her back and apologized.

"I don't know what came over me," Lara admitted. "I *am* happy for you. I just wish it was that easy for me."

Tiffany was confused.

"I'm sure Colin means to marry you. It's written all over his face. Has he ever asked you?"

"Well, not exactly, but I feel like he would, if I were ready. But I'm not. I wish I were."

Tiffany looked perplexed and Lara changed the subject.

"Let's not talk about Colin and me right now. I'm sure you have a story to tell me and I want to hear it."

Tiffany smiled widely. This was what she had hoped to hear.

Since Lara and Colin were in the same Sunday school class as Tiffany and Michael, they were invited to an engagement party for them. A year ago when Lara and Colin first began dating, there were several other singles or dating couples in their class. Now, for various reasons, Lara and Colin were the only ones who were unmarried and not engaged. This thought had not yet crossed Lara's mind. She wished it had because it might have made her more prepared and composed when it was brought up in conversation.

After most of the treats had been devoured, the focus turned to games. It was then that Mary, a bride of about six months, turned to Lara and said in a voice loud enough to be overheard by all,

"I guess it'll be your turn next."

Lara smiled as politely as she could, but said nothing. When she felt like all eyes were off her, she quietly left the room and headed outside. She knew Colin would come find her. She expected hearing him every second. After several minutes had passed, however, she began to wonder whether he had joined in the games without her. She didn't feel like playing anything now. She could only think of what had been said and wonder if everyone would be watching her and Colin and speculating about their future together. When she had almost forgotten to expect him, Colin appeared. He seemed annoyed and she thought she understood how he felt. But she quickly realized that his frustrations were different than her own.

"I've been thinking," he began slowly, "about your family reunion."

Lara quickly jumped to the wrong conclusion.

"You're not going to come?"

"No," he said quickly. "I never said that. I wish you wouldn't always think the worst of me." The hurt showed in Colin's eyes and, if Lara was feeling bad before, she felt much worse now.

"I'm sorry," she said numbly. "What were you going to say?"

Colin reached for her hands and held them in his for a moment before responding.

"I'm looking forward to spending this time with you and your family. But after the reunion is over, I need an answer. I want to plan for the future and I want you to be a part of that future. I can't always be riding the fence. We're already being teased."

"That's not a good reason to be rushing into marriage," Lara said.

"I didn't say it was, but we wouldn't be rushing things."

Lara searched Colin's eyes and saw his determination in them. She realized that if she wavered too long, she might lose him. And that thought scared her more than any of her fears could at that moment. She was thankful that Colin had given her a little more time, but now she knew how limited the time was.

"Okay," she agreed, smiling nervously.

Colin was pleased, although he wouldn't have minded a little more encouragement. After wrapping his arm around her, he led her back inside to the party. Lara had to endure a little more teasing before the evening was spent, but her mind was so absorbed in her earlier conversation with Colin, that it no longer troubled her.

A few weeks later, Colin celebrated a birthday. Although he wasn't particularly excited because it was a reminder that time was quickly passing. He told Lara to keep any plans she had for him simple and she had complied with his wishes. After dinner together, Lara handed him an envelope. She watched with interest as Colin opened it and pulled out two slips of paper.

"Rangers tickets! Thanks!" Colin's wide smile told Lara that he appreciated the gift she had chosen for him.

"I thought that I'd go with you, if you'd like." Lara made this offer in all sincerity, but Colin had to disfigure his face to keep from laughing out loud.

"You want to go to a baseball game?!"

Lara was almost annoyed, but she couldn't honestly say she had any desire to go to the game. She had been merely trying to strengthen their relationship by taking a greater interest in Colin's hobbies.

"Who would you rather take?" she asked at last.

"I thought about taking my nephew, Connor. I've been promising to have a guys' outing with him for some time."

"That sounds like it would be fun for both of you." Lara relaxed. She was actually relieved Colin didn't take her up on her offer.

"What made you offer to go in the first place? We both know that you would be bored."

"I didn't want there to be things that we can't share together," Lara admitted. She was feeling a little self-conscious.

"Well, if you'd like, I can tell you every detail of the game when I return. That would at least spare you the heat, noise, and sticky chair." Colin and Lara laughed easily. Then, Colin took Lara's hand in his and spoke in a more serious tone. "It means a lot to me that you care so much."

Lara blushed slightly. She was glad he had seen her heart,

even if she hadn't done the greatest job expressing herself.

Colin passed by the window once, then again. He didn't know what it was about entering this jewelry store that gave him hope. Maybe it was the mesmerizing cut of the diamonds or the way the employees treated you, like you had a reason to be there. Of course, that was their job. Still, he couldn't help just stepping inside for a quick peek at the ring he had spotted on his last visit.

Almost instantly the same employee approached him.

"Can I help you, Mr. Trent?"

Colin was momentarily speechless. How could she possibly know his name? He had never filled out anything and he was sure he'd never mentioned it on his last visit. Glancing down shyly, Colin noticed that he was still wearing his work badge on his pocket. Well, that would explain it.

"I... uh... was just looking," he mumbled awkwardly. As soon as another customer walked in and the employee looked away, Colin bolted out the door he'd entered just moments before. He determined not to set foot in this place again, unless he was really ready to buy a ring.

Daisy looked up from her magazine when she heard a knock on her door. She smiled when she caught sight of her unexpected visitor.

"Colin Trent! To what do I owe the pleasure of your company?"

"Well, Lara always tells me that you're the fount of wisdom. I wondered if I might trouble you for a little advice."

"It's no trouble. I'm happy to help if I can. What seems to be the matter?"

"I know Lara talks to you a lot. I imagine she told you about a conversation we had recently. We're getting ready to go to her family reunion together. I told her I wanted her to make her mind up about me by the end of the reunion. It seemed reasonable at the time, but now I wonder if it was a bad move."

Daisy nodded, taking in the situation. She really cared about Lara and Colin and wanted to see them together. She wasn't sure she was qualified to give unbiased advice, but she'd do her best.

"I can't say I know for sure if you said the right thing, but I do believe that God will use this for good for you and Lara. Sometimes we all need a little extra encouragement. I trust it will all work out. Just have faith."

"So you know that Colin and I will be leaving in two days to go to my family reunion?" Lara asked Daisy, obviously a little hesitant.

Daisy nodded, trying to repress a smile. First Colin, now Lara had come to see her. She sensed what was coming.

"I feel like something big is about to happen," Lara said, "I just don't know exactly what it will look like."

"You don't," Daisy agreed, "but God does."

"Pray for me?" Lara asked weakly.

"You can count on it," Daisy assured her.

"Thank you. I promise to tell you all about it when we get back."

"I'll look forward to it!"

Lara gave Daisy a hug and stood to leave.

"I've got a long list of things to do when I get home. I'd better get started on it."

"Have a good time!" Daisy said to Lara as she walked away.

As Lara packed for her family reunion, her feelings rose and fell, excitement and anxiety doing battle within her. She truly was looking forward to this trip. Perhaps it was because Colin was coming with her. Even though her relationship with him had not been smooth sailing of late, it was times like these when she realized how much she really had come to depend on him. He steadied her and helped her gather strength when she needed it. How strange that she needed strength to trust him with the rest of her life.

She also anticipated seeing her sister. She had often thought of Dee's visit in recent months. While Dee's direct way of talking made her sometimes nervous or annoyed, she knew that Dee meant well.

Colin was coming to pick her up in the morning and drive her to the airport. She knew that once they departed, she would have little time to herself until they returned. So, feeling the need for some time alone with her Heavenly Father, she knelt beside her bed, still heaped with folded laundry and toiletries, and prayed.

The sun was just beginning to rise above wispy clouds when Colin rang Lara's doorbell the following morning. Lara promptly appeared. She had quickly managed her morning routine and found herself prepared to leave more than half an hour ago. She smiled sweetly at Colin and was more thankful than ever for him.

Colin had spent the previous evening struggling with doubts about this trip. He felt it would either be the beginning of something wonderful or the end of it. In fact, his words with Lara had pretty much guaranteed one outcome or another.

As the sun shone on Lara's light brown hair and illuminated her smile, Colin felt something leap up inside of him. It was hope.

"So we're going to pick up Lara and Colin from the airport, right?" Joanne asked Aaron.

"That's the plan," Aaron said.

"I'm feeling a little nervous," Joanne admitted.

"About what?"

"About how to make Lara feel more comfortable with us. She likes to spend so much time by herself. I'd like to see that change."

"Well, she'll have Colin with her," Aaron said. "Maybe he'll be a help."

"Or maybe she'll be more distracted than ever!" Joanne said helplessly.

"We can only do our best to reach out to our daughter. At some point she'll have to reach back. You know, I hear that Colin is pretty serious about her. He may be wanting to talk to me sometime in the not too distant future."

"Where did you hear that?" Joanne asked, obviously surprised.

"Well, there's a saying, 'If you want *de*tails, ask Dee'".

"I've never heard that before in my life," Joanne said.

"I think I just made it up, but it suits our second daughter to a tee."

After a smooth first leg of their journey, Colin and Lara discovered that their connection had been delayed for two hours. After Lara notified her family not to expect them until later, she and Colin found seats in an airport deli and ordered some sandwiches.

Lara was surprised at how relaxed she felt. She had never enjoyed flying, but today she had thought less of the inconveniences than of the delights. She had probably never before spent so much time staring out the window during a flight, watching the clouds beneath her.

Colin too seemed to be in good spirits. He asked her many questions about their upcoming trip and whether Lara knew what her family might have planned for the week.

Lara knew that card games, catching crabs, and boating would surely be on the docket. Beyond that she really did not know. It occurred to her that she should tell Colin a little more about the extended members of her family that he would be seeing before the day was out.

"I was wondering when you would tell me about them. Did you think I would turn around and run away if you had enlightened me sooner?" Colin asked teasingly.

Lara smiled. She knew she deserved that question. She had been embarrassed, although the reasons why had less to do with her family members themselves and more to do with what they might say about *her*. Although Lara was now known for being quiet and reserved, as a child she had been quite animated and unpredictable at times. She hoped at least that the story of the chewing gum was not mentioned.

"My grandparents both passed away years ago. We've always missed them at our family reunions since. My great-aunt, Rosa, is in her late seventies now. She still drives and lives independently. I'm sure you'll enjoy meeting her."

"I'm sure I will."

"My mom's sister, Tabby, and her husband, Tom, and their two children, Grace and John, will be there. Grace and John are both in college now. I haven't seen them in a few years.

"Then there's my mom's brother, Sam, and his wife, Shelley, and their daughter, Emily. That's everyone."

"Anything special I should know about all these people you're introducing me to?"

Lara thought for a moment before responding. Her family was "normal" to her, but she tried to think of anything that would stand out to someone who hadn't before spent time with them.

"Well, my family tends to be loud. And I would steer clear of politics unless you want to be in a debate all night."

Colin surprised Lara by taking a small pad of paper and pen from his shirt pocket. He quickly scribbled something before looking up at her. She glanced down and read "no politics!"

"Are you taking notes?! You're not going to meet the Queen!"

"No," Colin answered smiling. "I'm going to meet your family, which is more important. The Queen would never remember me, but I hope to be known to your family for a long time."

Lara blushed. Colin would work his way into everyone's hearts this week. He had already found a way into hers.

Lara's parents were ready and waiting for her and Colin when their plane landed. Aaron James was quick to offer to help with the luggage, but his wife was engaged with talking to her

A Legacy for Lara

daughter and Colin. Lara was pleased that her mother welcomed Colin so enthusiastically. No doubt she hoped that Lara would marry before long.

"So what has Lara been telling you about us?" Aaron asked.

"Not too much," Colin answered, "but I will avoid any political speeches and I brought my ears plugs just in case."

Lara wasn't sure how her parents would react, but she relaxed when she saw their smiles.

"I'm not sure I wouldn't recommend those precautions in many places," her father said. He put his hand on Colin's shoulder to lead him out toward their vehicle. Lara followed with her mother, feeling that their time together was off to a decent start.

Dee was anxiously waiting back at the cabin for them. She had prepared dinner for everyone, with the help of Grace and Emily. Upon their arrival, she flew to the door, welcoming Lara and Colin both with open arms.

"I wanted to come to the airport, but I had kitchen duty tonight. How are you?"

"We're fine," Lara answered calmly, "a little tired, but fine."

Lara introduced Colin to each of her relatives. They were all kind in welcoming him, but he felt the awkwardness of being introduced as her boyfriend. He was the only one who didn't quite belong there. He hoped that might change before long.

Everyone was soon collected for dinner. Aaron offered to pray before their meal. Lara wasn't sure all of her relatives shared their practice of prayer, but no one made any objections. Lara was touched by the change in her father. She remembered his stern way of speaking to her as a child. Yet now his voice was soft and his manner of expression humble and thankful. She involuntarily brushed away a tear as Aaron gave thanks to the Lord for bringing them safely together. When she opened her eyes she saw Colin watching her closely. He gave her a smile of reassurance. It seemed odd that he should almost seem more at home with her family than she did herself. But then he appeared to be at home wherever she saw him. His behavior didn't alter much based on who he was with or where he was.

After dinner, Lara's parents rose to clean up. Colin stopped them, volunteering himself and Lara for the job.

"Are you sure you wouldn't rather rest?" Joanne asked.

"No, we'll be fine," Lara said. "Dinner was delicious and I wouldn't mind being on my feet after spending so much time sitting today."

Colin was glad that Lara thought the same way he did. He offered to wash the dishes while Lara dried them.

"You seem to be enjoying yourself a lot," Lara observed casually when she and Colin were alone in the kitchen together.

"That's because I am," he said. "Aren't you?"

"Yes, more than I expected. I think you make me see things differently than I used to."

"Good." Colin smiled. Lara blushed. She had been thinking about her relationship with her family, but she imagined Colin might be thinking of her relationship with him. As she thought of it, her statement was proving true in both cases, but she wasn't ready just yet to admit it.

The next morning after breakfast, Lara visited with her mother on the front porch.

"So how is your work going?" Joanne asked Lara.

A Legacy for Lara

"All right for the most part. Working with the public can be difficult at times."

"Care to elaborate?"

"Are you sure you really want me to?"

"Of course," Joanne answered.

"Well, I do my best to accommodate requests people make when I take their pictures, but some things are beyond my control. No matter how hard I try, I cannot make people look taller, slimmer, or younger than they really are."

"Do people really say those things to you?"

"Not always in those words. Some people like to drop hints, others speak pretty plainly. After taking pictures of subjects that like to find fault, you can see why I enjoy bringing my camera with me on vacation. I've never had the sunset tell me, 'You made me too fat.'"

Joanne was laughing and Lara found herself laughing too. Colin passed by the kitchen at that moment and saw the two women together. He winked at Lara and she smiled back.

Later that evening, when everyone was gathered together, Lara's cousin started the topic of conversation that Lara had been dreading.

"I know something fun that we can do!" Emily exclaimed. "We can tell family stories. And I know exactly which one I'm going to tell." Emily leaned closer to her cousin, John, and whispered, "The gum incident."

Lara was seated on the other side of the room. Before she realized what was happening or how to stop it, Emily had blurted out the embarrassing story. Even though time had taken some of the sting out of the memory, Lara still remembered how years ago, after getting her braces, she'd started chewing on some gum in the middle of a sucker. She hadn't been thinking really. The gum became stuck in her braces and it took some doing to get it all out. She never knew why her family members all found it so amusing. Apparently, time had not diminished the enjoyment that they had at her expense. If anything, it had increased it.

Lara hardly dared to look at Colin lest she see him laughing too. To her surprise, she heard him speak up in a clear, decided tone that helped to settle her jangled nerves.

"I fail to see the humor in the story," Colin began. "I assume that Lara could have messed her braces up and might have been in pain. But..." Colin's tone softened as he continued, "now I know why Lara has such a beautiful smile."

Colin reached for Lara's hand as he smiled at her. She couldn't help smiling back. It wasn't so bad being laughed at… not really. Not when you had someone to stand up for you.

Chapter Seven

Later that evening, Colin asked Lara if she had any interest in taking a boat out on the lake. The night was clear and there was still a little daylight left. Lara readily agreed and the two set off by themselves.

Lara brought her camera with her. She seemed to grab it more readily than her purse, Colin thought.

"Maybe instead of wearing necklaces, you should just wear your camera," he'd teased her in the past.

Lara especially liked to take pictures of water and sunsets. She snapped a few now, before turning to Colin with a pleased smile on her face.

"I want to thank you for standing up for me with my family," Lara said warmly. "I know they enjoy rehashing old stories and probably don't realize how uncomfortable they make me, but I really appreciated what you said. I was a little afraid you'd laugh at me like everyone else."

"Even if the whole world is laughing at you, I promise I won't be," Colin answered confidently.

"That means a lot to me."

"Can I ask you something, Lara?"

"Sure."

"What is it that you're really afraid of?"

"What do you mean?"

"I mean what makes you afraid about us? Sometimes if you can say a thing out loud you realize it's not as big of an obstacle as you thought it would be."

Lara hesitated. She wasn't sure she had ever determined her underlying fear before this moment, but it suddenly came to her.

"I think, what I struggle with is… our relationship right now is beautiful…"

"And that's a problem?" Colin interrupted, with a sly grin on his face.

Lara gave Colin an angry stare before answering his smile.

"You didn't let me finish! No, what I *meant* to say was… it seems like a lot of relationships start out beautiful, but somewhere down the road, they become the opposite. How can I know that we won't end up like that someday?"

Lara exhaled deeply. Her words had surprised even herself. She was glad that Colin didn't answer her right away. She could tell he was thinking, maybe even praying, for the words to form a response.

"Well, I guess a relationship is kind of like a garden."

"You're going to use a metaphor?"

"Now who's interrupting?"

"Sorry, my bad."

"Anyway, a garden is beautiful when you plant it, but if you just leave it to itself it won't stay that way. You have to weed it and water it and care for it all the time. I think relationships go downhill because they aren't maintained."

Colin let go of the oars, leaving them to drift ever so slightly on the water. He reached across for Lara's hand and looked deeply into her eyes. Lara had no thoughts of teasing now.

"I promise to make our relationship my highest priority, next to my relationship with God. I don't know if I can say anything else to reassure you, but I hope that this does."

Lara nodded her head as a few tears trickled down her cheeks. She wasn't sure what she had expected would finally put her fears to rest. This seemed to be what she had been searching for without knowing it.

When Lara and Colin returned to the cabin, Lara was surprised to see Emily apparently waiting for her.

"I feel really bad about what I said. I'm sorry," Emily blurted out all in one breath. "I like to make people laugh, but I should never have been trying to make them laugh *at you*. Forgive me?"

"Of course," Lara assured her. She had already forgiven Emily and forgotten the incident. She had too many other things on her mind just now to worry about a little teasing. She was thinking about what Colin had said to her tonight and about the answer she would give him at the end of the week.

"By the way," Emily continued, interrupting Lara's thoughts, "I think it was really great how Colin stood up for you. I hope someday I'll find someone who will stand up for me like that."

Lara smiled and gave Emily a hug.

"I hope you do too."

It was Wednesday, and although Daisy tried to find interest in the book she was reading, her mind kept traveling miles away. She thought of Lara and Colin and prayed for them yet again. She hoped that the time they were spending together would accomplish more than one object. She wished to see Lara become closer to her family and she hoped that Lara would overcome her fears and finally encourage Colin's hope of marriage.

She had tried as best as she could to help Lara see that her fears demonstrated a lack of faith, in Colin and in God. With a sudden inspiration she wondered if it would be easier for her to share her thoughts in a letter. Lara would not receive it until she returned when, perhaps, her relationship with Colin would already have been changed for the better or the worse. But Daisy felt determined to try.

She found some stationery and a pen and began writing *Dear Lara.* The words seemed to come in quick succession as though she had been holding them back and now they burst forth from her pen. Then a verse of Scripture came to mind and she wondered why it had never occurred to her before. She felt more than ever that her interference was warranted and that, perhaps, God would use it for good in Lara's life.

When at last her letter was complete, she sealed it and put it aside. Then, feeling weary, she asked for assistance to ready herself for a good night's sleep.

The next day at the beach house, Lara and her family were having a leisurely breakfast. Suddenly, Lara's phone rang out a merry tune that little foretold what was to come.

"Hold that thought," Lara said, reaching to retrieve her phone. "Hello?"

Colin watched with increasing anxiety as Lara's face went pale while tears began to form in her eyes and she looked unseeing past him to the lake beyond.

"Yes, I'm still here. Thank you for letting me know." A few more moments passed silently while Lara seemed to be struggling to understand what was being told to her. "I'll make new arrangements right away."

The silence hung in the air. Lara didn't know how she managed to express the words, but she did.

"Daisy passed away in her sleep last night."

Chapter Eight

"You know what really makes me feel bad?" Lara asked Colin. He merely shrugged in response.

"I never got to tell Daisy how much I appreciated her," Lara choked on her tears, "or how much she meant to me."

Colin laid his hand on Lara's shoulder. Lara's head was bent low now and the tears fell unchecked onto her floral skirt.

"You may not have told her in words," Colin answered steadily, his voice convincing and sure. "But she knew that you cared about her. You were there, every week, checking on her, encouraging her."

For a moment, Lara's grief seemed to lessen. Then a fresh torrent of tears came pouring forth. Lara shook visibly, seemingly more upset than she was at the first.

"Lara, what is it?" Colin asked, concerned that he had unknowingly caused her added distress.

Lara made an attempt to dry her tears. She knew she needed to tell him what was on her heart, but wondered if she could get the words out.

"Could we take a walk along the beach?" she asked weakly. Colin had to lean close to her to catch her words. He wished with all his heart that he could take away her suffering. Yet, he was relieved that she was making this request of him, however small. He hoped that when they returned to the beach house she would be more at ease and able to sleep well before their journey home the following morning.

"You were right when you said that Daisy knew how much I cared about her," Lara said softly to Colin. They were holding hands and walking along the shore.

"So you should be encouraged, right?" Colin asked, hoping to cheer her a little.

"Yes…and no," Lara answered. "I'm so thankful that I met Daisy. We had a special relationship and I'll never forget her. But when I think about my family…"

Colin began to put the puzzle pieces together in his mind before Lara was calm enough to finish her explanation.

"I've pushed them away, Colin. I've spent more time with someone I only met a few years ago than I have with my parents and my sister. Everyone saw it… except for me. How could I have been so blind? If something had happened to one of my family members, would they have known that I cared about them?"

Lara stopped walking as she gave in to her grief and remorse. Colin wrapped his arms around Lara while her tears flowed freely. For a few minutes neither spoke. Then Lara looked up into Colin's eyes, a searching look on her face.

"And you…"

"Me?" Colin asked puzzled.

"Yes. You've been so good to me," Lara answered. "I've spent all this time asking myself if I could trust you."

Colin was glad that Lara had once again looked away. He was afraid his eyes might betray the hurt her words caused him.

"Now I wonder," Lara began again, "why I never stopped to ask if I could trust my own judgment. I've been so afraid. I've been so wrong. I'm sorry."

"I forgive you," Colin answered easily. "I'm sure your family will too."

Lara nodded slowly. A smile was beyond her strength for the moment, but she let Colin's words sink into her heart. She needed to talk to her family and make things right. She realized how thankful she was that she was being given this opportunity. Daisy and Colin had always encouraged her to reach out to her family. Now she was finally listening.

"I can't say how thankful I am that you came here." Lara's words were softly spoken, but Colin heard and treasured each one. "I don't know what I would have done without you."

"Well…" Colin said, searching for something to say. As he hesitated, he looked at the scenery around him. The sun was beginning to set and the sky had erupted in shades of orange, red, and yellow that reflected in the water below. Gulls flew overhead, talking to one another. The beauty of it seemed to give him courage. "I hope to never be far away from you."

Lara was stunned. She was beginning to feel how very undeserving she was of the regard that others had for her. Colin's words made her feel weak at the knees. How had she ever doubted him? Now she could only ask herself what she had ever done to attract him. He was too good for her. He was consistent and confident, forgiving and faithful. All the things she wished she had been and still hoped she could be.

"Thank you," she said meekly. "I think I had better turn in early so I can be ready for my flight tomorrow."

"*Our* flight," Colin corrected. For some reason, Lara had envisioned flying home on her own. It seemed silly now. Of course Colin would come with her. He had no reason to stay now that she was leaving.

"Yes, our flight," she repeated. "I don't think I'll be very good company, but I'll appreciate you being there." Lara was beginning to see how much she depended on Colin and how dependable he really was.

The next morning as Lara prepared her suitcase, she also mentally prepared what she would say to her family before she left. She had thought about it off and on during the night. Even though she'd gone to bed before ten o'clock, she'd only managed to get a few hours of sleep. The sadness of losing Daisy, the self-reproach she felt, and the remembrance of Colin's kindness kept her mind swirling in a steady stream. Some thoughts lifted her to the highest heights, while others plunged her to depths she had never before known.

Later that morning, all Lara's extended family members made themselves scarce so that Lara could have a few quiet moments with her immediate family.

"Mom, Dad, Dee..." Lara acknowledged each member of her family with a nod. "As you know, I've been struggling since I heard about Daisy."

"Of course," Joanne answered understandingly.

"But I've been struggling for another reason too. I told Colin that I regretted not having told Daisy how much she meant to me. He told me that I did tell her, in my actions. I was there to encourage her." Tears began to pool in Lara's eyes. "I got to thinking that three years ago, I met Daisy for the first time. But I showed her how much she meant to me by being there. But I've known you all my life, and I've pushed you away. If something happened to any of you, I..." Lara could not continue her thought, but it wasn't necessary. Before she realized what had happened, she found herself engulfed in the arms of her mother, father, and sister.

"I'm so sorry..."

While they were huddled together, Aaron began to pray for

his family. He prayed for Lara's and Colin's safety and for their comfort in the loss of Daisy. Lara was truly amazed at the transformation in her father. She had lacked faith; she saw that now.

"I'm so sorry about Daisy," Dee began. "I'm really glad I had the chance to meet her. She was a special lady."

"She told me I should have made more of an effort to keep in touch with you," Lara admitted. "I wish I had listened to her sooner. Daisy gave me so much good advice and lots of good memories."

"It sounds like she left you quite the legacy," Dee remarked.

"Yeah," Lara nodded slowly, "all I could ever hope for… and more.

"I'll keep in touch," Lara promised.

"I'll count on it!" Dee answered.

Chapter Nine

The return flight home behind them, Colin led Lara up to her door. She hesitated before going inside.

"Colin, I know that I said that I would have an answer for you, but with all that's going on…"

Colin placed his hands gently on Lara's shoulders.

"It's okay, Lara," Colin said quickly. "I understand. I wish you trusted me a little more so that you didn't feel like you needed to explain yourself. I wasn't going to bring it up."

"Oh," Lara said. She felt foolish for her words and wished now she could take them back.

"Why don't you go get some sleep, hmm?" Colin leaned closer to Lara and brushed the hair away from her face. "I love you, Lara," he whispered in her ear.

Lara stood transfixed for a moment. This was the first time that Colin had ever said he loved her and she was speechless. It took her a second to realize that Colin had turned and started to walk away.

"Colin, wait!" Lara took a few steps and nearly crashed into Colin, who had stopped immediately. She looked up at him and smiled.

"I love you too."

Colin once again held Lara against his chest. Inwardly he was asking himself why he had ever given Lara an ultimatum in the first place. Sure, he wanted to be married soon, but he wanted to be married to *her*. This evening gave him hope that maybe both might soon become a reality.

Lara had unpacked from her trip, then collapsed on the sofa. She couldn't help thinking about Daisy, Colin, and her family. The telephone brought Lara's torrent of thoughts to a standstill.

"Is this Lara James?" said an unknown caller.

"Yes."

"I'm Ivy from the Senior Care Facility. When Daisy Jenkins' room was being cleaned, there was a letter found for you. Could you please come by at your earliest convenience to pick it up?"

"Yes, I suppose I can do that."

As Lara pulled up in front of the familiar building, she felt a pang in her chest. She turned off the engine and dropped her keys into her purse. Taking a deep breath, Lara prayed for the strength she would need to make it through this.

Inside the lobby, Lara approached the desk where she was told a letter was waiting for her. Apparently Daisy had written and addressed a letter to Lara, but it was never mailed, presumably because Daisy wrote it the night before she died.

The woman at the counter quickly retrieved the letter for Lara and told her she was sorry for her loss. Lara thanked her numbly, then turned away to hide the tears that had begun to form in her eyes. Looking at the envelope, she lovingly fingered the words that Daisy had written. She would not read them here. Tonight, with a cup of tea and plenty of tissues she would read the last words she would ever hear from Daisy.

Lara wished she could leave now, but she was told that

Daisy's roommate, Flo, had asked to see her. Lara hated the thought of stepping foot into Daisy's room and not finding Daisy there, but she knew she needed to listen to the older woman. Daisy would have wanted it.

When Lara stepped inside Room 26, and saw how bare Daisy's place had become, she felt she could not control her emotions. Perhaps she should plan to visit Flo another day. Maybe it was all too much too quick.

"Lara? Is that you?"

Lara looked further into the room to see Flo with a look of expectation on her face. Swallowing her tears, Lara stepped forward.

"Yes, I'm here."

"Thank you for coming." Lara had never heard Flo speak so much at one time. Clearly she too had been affected by losing her roommate, if not her friend.

"I imagine you're mighty shaken by the loss of Daisy," Flo began. "I know I am. I treated her cruelly. All she ever wanted to do was to be my friend." Now Flo was crying in earnest. Lara handed her a box of tissues. Suddenly inspired by a memory she had nearly forgotten, Lara knew what to say to ease Flo's mind.

"You would never have known this," Lara began, "but my first impression of Daisy was very different than what you might expect."

Their first meeting had been far from promising. In fact, Lara left that day uncertain if she would ever return to Room 26. But something had beckoned to her underneath the older woman's cold exterior. Something she had seen inside herself. A barrier erected to protect against pain and disappointment. Lara was forever thankful that she had not stayed away.

Her pastor had told her of a widow who had just seen her

hadn't known Daisy all her life. She had come to rely on her sound advice and loved listening to the stories Daisy told of her younger days.

"You're a good storyteller," Flo admitted, when Lara had finished her narrative. "It is all true, right?"

"Every bit. You can ask Pastor Paul if you don't believe me."

"Maybe Daisy and I had more in common than I realized." Flo was quiet for a moment. "Just out of curiosity… what will you be doing with your Wednesday afternoons now?"

Lara hadn't exactly considered this question before. She looked at Flo's hopeful expression, and, as she did so, the light broke from behind the clouds and Flo appeared wreathed in sunlight.

"I'll be here." Lara said without hesitation. It was where she was meant to be.

Chapter Ten

Dear Lara,

I hope this letter finds you well and enjoying time with your family
and Colin. I must admit I'm praying you two will come to an understanding while you are away and have happy news to share with me
upon your return. I wanted to share this verse with you. You may be
familiar with it, but I'm praying the Holy Spirit will help you see it with fresh eyes and in light of your current struggle.

There is no fear in love; but perfect love casts out fear, because fear involves punishment, and the one who fears is not perfected in love. 1 John 4:18

You may remember a time when I too struggled with fear of rejection.
You must remember how cold I was to you when we first met. I feared you were merely trying to do a good deed or get some bonus points for volunteering to help you find a
job. I almost missed out on the joy of knowing you. You know Reg
and I could never have children. I've never told you this before, but
I've often thought of you as a granddaughter.

I'm growing tired so I feel I must conclude. Remember this: when we

let go of something we've been holding on to and let God do His work,
it's often more wonderful than we can imagine.

Love,
Daisy

Lara read the letter through at least three times before deciding on a course of action. Then she was sure. She called Colin and asked him to come over that evening.

"There was no one quite like Daisy," Colin said, handing the letter back to Lara. Lara accepted it and carefully placed it in her purse. At the same time, she pulled out a tissue and reached to dry her eyes.

"And there never will be," she said quietly. "I'm sorry; I know that someday I'll be able to talk about her without crying, but... not today."

Colin reached for Lara's free hand and wrapped his around it.

"That's okay." Both were silent for a few moments, then Colin spoke up again. "So, can I ask why you had me read that letter? It was pretty personal. I wouldn't have read it if you hadn't insisted."

Lara hesitated. Of course, she was going to tell him her reason, but she had intended to pace her conversation. Was she ready now to tell him everything?

"Well, I thought you should know that Daisy was thinking of you on the last day of her life."

"I appreciate that," Colin said slowly, "but something tells me that's only part of your reason. After all, you could have told me as much without having me read the letter."

Lara felt trapped. Colin was smart and he knew her well. She should have anticipated as much.

"You're right," she admitted. "I had another motive. I wanted you to read the letter so that you would understand me when I tell you that… I'm not afraid anymore. Do you know what I mean when I say that?"

"Possibly, but so there's no misunderstanding…" Colin's words trailed off and Lara quickly filled the silence.

"All that time that I doubted you, you were showing me in every possible way that I could trust you. I see that now. I'm sorry I didn't see it sooner. I know I once became upset when you talked about our future together. But now… I can't imagine my future without you. I don't even want to try."

"Are you saying…" Colin stopped himself abruptly. Was he really hearing what he thought he was hearing? Impatient to learn more, he asked quickly, "Are you saying that you'll marry me?"

"That's exactly what I'm saying," Lara said.

Colin didn't even hesitate outside the door this time. He walked boldly in, intent on his purpose.

"Good afternoon, Mr. Trent. How are you today?"

Colin wondered inwardly if it was a good thing to be known by name at a jewelry store. No matter, today he had actual business to attend to.

"I've come to purchase that ring I've looked at a few times in the past."

"Splendid! I know exactly which one you're referring to." The sales assistant led Colin to the familiar glass case. He watched as she unlocked the glass and removed the ring. "This is it, correct?"

"That's the one."

"And may I ask who's the lucky lady?"

"My fiancée."

"Oh? Generally the ring is given at the time of engagement."

"Well, I didn't know we'd be getting engaged yesterday, so I didn't know to have a ring ready."

"You didn't know you were going to propose yesterday?"

"Well, it's a little more complicated than that…" Colin didn't know why he'd said as much as he had. He was tempted to flee to another jewelry store and never look back. But he felt Lara would appreciate this ring more than any other he had seen.

"Do you get a discount if you pay in cash?" Colin loved watching the look on the assistant's face. Clearly she would have liked to hear more of his story, but she couldn't afford to offend her customer.

"Why don't we walk over to the register?"

The phone rang and Lara reached to answer it.
"Hello?"

"How's my wife-to-be?"
"You seem to enjoy saying that," Lara said. After all her hesitation, she was surprised at how natural all this seemed.

"I was wondering if you might want to get out tonight and get ice cream."

"I would, but I'm kind of in the middle of something."

"Am I allowed to know what it is?"

"I suppose, but I want it to be a surprise for my parents. I'm editing pictures of the family vacation."

"Seems to me I remember suggesting that." Colin hoped he didn't sound smug. He was really glad that Lara had taken his advice on this. He knew she had taken some beautiful pictures on their trip. He couldn't wait to see them himself.

"Why don't you give me half an hour to wrap things up?" Lara suggested. "I can always work on these another day."

Later, as Lara and Colin sat outside eating ice cream, Colin told Lara something that surprised her.

"Did you ever know that I occasionally went to visit Daisy too?"

"No, she never said."

"I didn't go regularly like you; but if I was feeling discouraged, it was always fun to talk to her."

"And what did you have to feel discouraged about?" Lara asked, trying to appear unaware.

"Well, there was this girl that I really cared about who just couldn't make up her mind about me."

"Really?" Lara put her hand up to her mouth just in time to cover her giggle. Then she sobered. "I really am sorry I put you through that."

Colin leaned over to kiss Lara. "I know. I'm sure you can make it up to me."

Lara blushed.

"We are gathered here today to remember a great lady, Mrs. Daisy Jenkins." Lara barely heard another word of the service until she saw Flo wheel herself up to the front of the crowd. An audible gasp of surprise went forth as she did so. Everyone knew Flo to be a reticent woman who barely ever spoke. The room was uncommonly quiet as she prepared herself.

"For those of you who don't know me, I'm Flo. I was Daisy's roommate." Flo paused for breath. "You may say that I had quite the privilege and I don't disagree with you. But I didn't see it right away. And I never told her how much she meant to me.

"Once Daisy saw I wasn't much interested in talking, she started praying out loud at night for me. I listened every time. She had faith, Daisy did. She knew she was being heard. I almost stopped her once. I wanted to say 'don't waste your breath on me', but I didn't really mean it. So I didn't say it.

"I wished I would have thanked Daisy, but you see, I've lost my chance. If there's someone in your life who has helped you, please thank them. For my sake. Kindness shouldn't be taken for granted. Thank you."

Lara clapped loudly as Flo wheeled herself back to the crowd, then she gathered her notes.

"My name is Lara James. I met Daisy for the first time several years ago. I was looking to spend my Wednesday afternoons in a way that would benefit others, and Pastor Paul suggested that I begin visiting Daisy. She had attended our church faithfully before she was confined to a wheelchair.

"Daisy had been feeling discouraged because her last local relative had moved away and she was feeling alone. I wonder if any of you are feeling that way today.

"You may not have known it to look at her, but Daisy was rich. She didn't have gold and jewels, but she had wisdom. She trusted in Christ as her Savior as a young girl, and for more than sixty years, she walked with God.

"There were so many things she said to me that challenged me, encouraged me, and changed me. She had a unique perspective on life. Her influence helped me to forgive and to ask for forgiveness.

"Daisy told me about how her prayers had been answered throughout her life. I believe we've seen an answer to prayer this very day." At this, Lara nodded at Flo and noticed that the tears in her eyes reflected those in her own.

"I have asked Pastor Paul if we could sing her favorite hymn in closing. Please join me in singing, 'What a Friend We Have in Jesus!'"

Epilogue

"Aaron, there's a package here from Lara!" Joanne yelled as she came in the front door.

"Well, then open it!"

Aaron watched with interest as Joanne cut open the seal and pulled out an envelope full of pictures.

"These are beautiful!" Joanne gasped. "Oh, look here!"

"That's a nice picture!" Aaron commented. One of the relatives had been commissioned to take this picture since it was of Lara, Dee, both her parents, and Colin.

"This was what I prayed for!" Joanne exclaimed, momentarily stunned.

"I thought you wanted a picture with the four of us," Aaron answered.

"Well, sometimes God gives you more than you asked for."

Made in the USA
Lexington, KY
02 June 2019